The Final Level

Michael Ferguson

Published by Michael Ferguson, 2024.

THE FINAL LEVEL

First edition. August 14, 2024.

Copyright © 2024 Michael Ferguson.

ISBN: 979-8227959454

Written by Michael Ferguson.

Table of Contents

Chapter 1: The Gamers' Dream 1

Chapter 2: Offers on the Table 8

Chapter 3: The Pressure Builds 13

Chapter 4: The Cost Of Fame 18

Chapter 5: Building Trust 23

Chapter 6: Tournament Trials 27

Chapter 7: The Turning Point 31

Chapter 8: The Dilemma Intensifies 35

Chapter 9: The Breaking Point 39

Chapter 10: New Beginnings 44

Chapter 11: The Rewards of Integrity 48

Chapter 12: The Final Level 52

Chapter 1: The Gamers' Dream

Alex Carter's world revolved around the pixelated universe of Battalion Blitz, a high-octane online game that had taken the gaming community by storm. At sixteen, Alex was not just another teenager; he was a top-ranked player in a global competition where the stakes were high, and the spotlight was blinding. His handle, "AceStriker," was known across forums and streams, his name synonymous with skill and precision. Yet, despite his rising fame in the virtual world, his real-life situation was starkly different.

In the small, cluttered bedroom that served as both his sanctuary and his battleground, Alex sat hunched over his aging computer. The screen flickered occasionally, a relic of the many gaming marathons it had endured. The keyboard, worn from countless hours of frantic keystrokes, and the mouse, its surface chipped from relentless clicks, were the only signs of his dedication. The room itself was a makeshift shrine to his gaming passion—walls plastered with posters of his favorite eSports teams, shelves crowded with game-related memorabilia, and a small, fraying couch in the corner where he often slumped after long sessions.

Despite the apparent devotion, there was an undeniable divide between his aspirations and reality. Alex's family struggled financially, and the cost of high-quality streaming equipment, which was essential for a professional gamer, was far beyond their reach. His parents worked tirelessly, but their combined income barely covered the essentials. The dream of becoming a pro gamer seemed perpetually out of reach, a cruel irony given how close he was to the pinnacle of success in Battalion Blitz.

His days were a mix of school and gaming, a delicate balance that required intense focus and discipline. At school, Alex was an average student, not because he lacked intelligence but because his mind was always elsewhere—on strategies, game mechanics, and his next big move. His teachers and peers were aware of his gaming prowess, but few truly understood the depth of his dedication or the obstacles he faced. They saw him as a kid with a hobby, not realizing that for Alex, gaming was not just a pastime but a lifeline, a path to a future he yearned for.

Evenings were his sanctuary. As dusk fell, Alex would lock himself away in his room, the soft hum of his computer the only sound accompanying him. He would immerse himself in Battalion Blitz, where he was not just a player but a master strategist, a tactician who could bend the game's mechanics to his will. His in-game persona, AceStriker, was a hero in the digital realm, admired by fans and feared by opponents. Yet, behind the screen, Alex was just a teenager grappling with the harsh realities of life.

The financial constraints were a constant source of frustration. Alex had to make do with what he had—an outdated computer, a basic headset, and minimal accessories. His setup lacked the finesse and power of professional gear, and every time he lagged or faced technical difficulties during critical moments, it was a harsh reminder of the barriers standing between him and his dreams. The desire for an upgraded system was almost an obsession. He'd spend hours researching the latest equipment, watching unboxing videos, and reading reviews, wishing he could afford even a fraction of the gear that could enhance his performance.

His predicament became even more poignant when he watched other gamers rise to prominence. Streams of high-profile players with pristine setups and massive followings were a constant reminder of the gap between his current state and his aspirations. Alex knew that breaking into the professional scene required more than just skill—it needed visibility, quality equipment, and a platform to showcase his talents. But without the financial backing, his potential remained largely untapped.

Despite these challenges, Alex's dedication never wavered. His gameplay was exceptional, a blend of instinctive skill and learned strategies that made him a formidable opponent. His rise through the ranks of Battalion Blitz was a testament to his hard work and perseverance. He participated in online tournaments, often placing in the top ten, which provided a glimmer of hope that his efforts could one day pay off.

One evening, after an intense tournament where Alex narrowly missed the top spot, he slumped in his chair, exhausted but exhilarated. The victory would have meant more recognition, perhaps even an opportunity to connect with sponsors. Instead, it was another reminder of how close he was to achieving his dreams, yet how far he remained from making them a reality. He stared at the leaderboard, his name shining brightly but not quite at the top, and sighed deeply.

The room's door creaked open, and his younger sister, Lily, peeked in. At twelve, she was already showing signs of the same inquisitive nature and creativity that Alex admired. She had her own small corner in the room, where she kept her sketchbooks and art supplies. "How'd it go?" she asked, her voice filled with genuine curiosity.

"Not bad," Alex replied, forcing a smile. "Came close, but there's always next time."

Lily nodded, stepping inside. "I made you some cookies," she said, holding out a small plate. "I thought you might need a break."

Alex took the plate, touched by her thoughtfulness. "Thanks, Lil. You're the best."

As he munched on the cookies, Lily sat down on the couch, her eyes bright with admiration. "Do you think you'll ever get to be a pro gamer? Like, really famous?"

Alex hesitated, the question stirring a mix of hope and doubt. "I hope so," he said finally. "I just need a bit of luck and maybe some help."

Lily looked thoughtful. "Maybe you'll get it. You're really good, Alex. I believe in you."

Her faith was a small but significant source of motivation. As he watched her leave, Alex felt a renewed sense of determination. He knew that achieving his dream required more than just skill—it required resources, support, and perhaps a bit of serendipity. Little did he know that his life was about to change in ways he hadn't anticipated.

Alex Carter was at his desk, immersed in his latest gaming session, when his computer pinged with an incoming email. He glanced at the screen and saw two new messages waiting. The subject lines were intriguing: "Exciting Opportunity for AceStriker!" and "A Chance to Elevate Your Gaming Career." His pulse quickened as he clicked open the first email.

The message was from Victor Kline, a well-known name in the gaming community. Victor was known for discovering and nurturing top talent, and his name was often associated with breakthrough success stories. The email was a mix of formal and enthusiastic, outlining an offer that seemed almost too good to be true.

"Dear Alex,

Congratulations on your impressive performance in Battalion Blitz! Your skills have caught our eye, and we would like to offer you an incredible opportunity. As a top player in the global rankings, we believe you have the potential to become a gaming sensation.

Our company, Vortex Gaming, is prepared to provide you with state-of-the-art streaming equipment, promotional support, and access to a network of industry professionals. With our backing, you'll have the tools and exposure needed to reach new heights in your career.

However, to partner with us, we require a percentage of your future earnings and winnings. We believe this is a fair exchange for the extensive resources and connections we provide. If you're interested in discussing this further, please let us know at your earliest convenience.

Best regards,
Victor Kline
Vortex Gaming"

Alex's heart raced as he read through the offer. The promise of top-notch equipment and industry connections was enticing. It was the opportunity he had been dreaming of, the chance to transition from a talented amateur to a recognized professional. Yet, the mention of a percentage of his earnings was a caveat that he knew he would have to consider carefully.

He closed the email and opened the second one. This message was from Jamie Ruiz, a lesser-known figure but one with a reputation for supporting emerging talent with genuine dedication. Jamie's email was straightforward but filled with sincerity.

"Hi Alex,

I'm Jamie Ruiz, and I've been following your progress in Battalion Blitz. Your gameplay is outstanding, and I'm reaching out to offer you a different kind of support. While I may not have the same level of influence as some others, I'm passionate about helping promising players like you reach their potential.

I can offer you the equipment you need to start streaming professionally and guidance to navigate the competitive gaming scene. My terms are simple: I would take a minimal cut of your earnings, ensuring you keep the majority of what you earn. I'm committed to providing the support you need without overwhelming you with demands.

If this sounds like something you'd be interested in, let's chat about how we can work together to help you achieve your goals.

Best,

Jamie Ruiz"

As Alex finished reading Jamie's email, he felt a mix of relief and anxiety. Jamie's offer was straightforward and less demanding, but it lacked the immediate glamour of Victor's proposal. The idea of keeping more of his earnings was appealing, but the lack of an extensive network and promotional power was a significant drawback.

The two offers presented Alex with a dilemma that went beyond financial considerations. On one hand, Victor's offer came with the potential for rapid success and exposure, albeit at a cost. On the other hand, Jamie's offer promised a more supportive and sustainable partnership, with fewer immediate advantages but a fairer share of his earnings.

The next few days were a whirlwind for Alex. He spent hours weighing his options, researching Vortex Gaming and Jamie Ruiz, and discussing the offers with his family. His parents, though supportive, were uncertain. They saw the potential in both offers but struggled to grasp the implications of each.

"Victor Kline's offer seems incredible, Alex," his mother said one evening as they sat around the kitchen table. "But are you sure about giving up a large percentage of your earnings? It sounds like a lot."

Alex nodded, understanding her concern. "I know, Mom. It's a tough choice. Jamie's offer is fairer, but I'd be missing out on the exposure that Victor's offer provides."

His father, who had been quietly listening, spoke up. "You've always been dedicated to your gaming, Alex. Whatever choice you make, it needs to align with your long-term goals and values. Don't rush into anything just because it sounds glamorous."

The weight of their advice settled heavily on Alex's shoulders. He knew his family had his best interests at heart, but the decision was ultimately his to make. He spent long hours in his room, researching and contemplating the future. He watched videos of successful gamers who had partnered with both major organizations and smaller, supportive managers. He read interviews and testimonials, trying to gather as much information as possible.

During this period of reflection, Alex's gaming performance began to reflect his internal struggle. He found himself less focused during matches, making uncharacteristic mistakes and struggling to maintain his usual high level of play. The pressure of the decision was taking a toll on him, and he was acutely aware that his current performance might influence the outcome of his decision.

One evening, after a particularly challenging game session, Alex slumped into his chair and stared at the emails from Victor and Jamie. He knew that his decision would not only affect his career but also his personal values and future opportunities. The choice between rapid success and fair support was one that would shape his path in ways he couldn't yet fully understand.

As he contemplated his next steps, Alex realized that the decision was about more than just financial terms. It was about the kind of career he wanted to build, the relationships he wanted to foster, and the values he wanted to uphold. The offers were more than mere contracts—they were representations of different paths he could take, each with its own set of consequences.

Chapter 2: Offers on the Table

Alex Carter felt a mix of excitement and anxiety as he prepared for his video call with Victor Kline. The living room in his modest apartment was cluttered with old gaming equipment, a few posters of gaming legends, and a small desk where Alex had spent countless hours honing his skills in Battalion Blitz. He set up his webcam and adjusted the lighting, trying to make the space look as professional as possible, despite the limited resources.

When the call connected, Victor Kline appeared on the screen. Victor's polished appearance and confident demeanor instantly conveyed his high status in the gaming world. He wore a sleek, dark jacket over a branded gaming shirt, and his background was a well-designed studio with multiple screens displaying gaming graphics and statistics. The contrast between Victor's environment and Alex's setup was stark, but Alex forced himself to stay focused.

"Hello, Alex," Victor began, his voice smooth and authoritative. "It's a pleasure to finally meet you. I've been following your gameplay for a while now, and I must say, you're one of the most impressive young talents I've seen in a long time."

"Thank you, Mr. Kline," Alex replied, trying to keep his voice steady. "I'm honored to be speaking with you."

Victor leaned back in his chair and steepled his fingers. "Let's get right to it. As you know, Battalion Blitz is a game with immense potential, and we believe you have what it takes to become a top player. Our organization, Vortex Gaming, is prepared to offer you a comprehensive package that will elevate your career to the next level."

Alex's heart raced as he listened. Victor continued, outlining the details of the offer with enthusiasm.

"We'll provide you with state-of-the-art streaming equipment, including high-definition cameras, advanced microphones, and professional-grade lighting. Additionally, we'll manage your promotion and marketing, ensuring you gain the visibility you deserve in the gaming community. Our network of influencers and sponsors will give you the exposure you need to attract a large audience and secure sponsorships."

Victor paused for a moment, allowing the information to sink in. "However, as with any investment, there is a cost. We require a significant percentage of your future earnings and winnings. This percentage will be detailed in the contract, but I assure you that our support and resources will outweigh the financial commitment."

Alex nodded, though his mind was racing. The offer was undoubtedly impressive. The thought of having access to top-tier equipment and gaining exposure through Vortex Gaming was tempting. It was the kind of opportunity that could make a huge difference in his career, but the cost was something he would need to seriously consider.

Victor's gaze was steady as he continued. "I understand this is a lot to take in, but I want you to know that we are committed to seeing you succeed. Our goal is to help you reach the highest levels of competitive gaming. If you're interested, we can discuss the specifics of the contract and how we can get started."

Alex took a deep breath. "I appreciate the offer, Mr. Kline. It's a lot to think about, but I'm definitely interested in learning more about the terms."

Victor smiled, clearly pleased with Alex's response. "Excellent. I'll have our legal team send you a detailed contract outlining the percentage and other terms. Once you've reviewed it, we can discuss any questions you might have."

As the call ended, Alex sat back in his chair, feeling a mix of exhilaration and apprehension. The opportunity was extraordinary, but the cost was significant. He knew he had to weigh his options carefully.

Later that evening, as Alex reviewed the initial details of Victor's offer, he couldn't shake the excitement of the potential opportunity. The high-profile support could be a game-changer for his career, but he also felt a pang of unease about the financial terms. He needed to consider how the offer would impact his long-term goals and whether it aligned with his personal values.

The next day, Alex received an email from Jamie Ruiz, the smaller-scale manager who had also expressed interest in helping him. Jamie's offer was less flashy but came with a personal touch that contrasted sharply with the corporate feel of Victor's proposal. As Alex opened Jamie's email, he braced himself for another round of contemplation and decision-making.

The email from Jamie Ruiz was a stark contrast to the high-stakes pitch from Victor Kline. Jamie's message was warm and personal, reflecting a genuine passion for gaming and a sincere desire to support Alex's growth. After reading through the email, Alex felt a sense of relief from the formality and corporate nature of Victor's offer. He decided to set up a call with Jamie to discuss the opportunity further.

When the video call connected, Jamie Ruiz appeared on the screen. Jamie looked relaxed and approachable, sitting in a room decorated with gaming memorabilia and a few cozy touches, like a beanbag and a small collection of game controllers. Jamie's easygoing demeanor made Alex feel immediately at ease.

"Hey, Alex," Jamie greeted with a friendly smile. "Thanks for taking the time to chat. I've been following your progress in Battalion Blitz, and I'm really impressed with what you've achieved so far."

"Hi, Jamie. Thank you for reaching out. I'm excited to hear more about what you're offering," Alex replied, his curiosity piqued.

Jamie nodded and began outlining the offer. "So, I run a smaller gaming management agency called NextGen Gamers. We might not have the same level of influence as Vortex Gaming, but we pride ourselves on providing personalized support to our clients. Here's what we can offer you: we'll help you with access to high-quality streaming equipment, including cameras, microphones, and lighting. More importantly, we'll work closely with you to build your brand and grow your audience."

Alex listened attentively as Jamie continued. "What sets us apart is our hands-on approach. We'll be there every step of the way, offering guidance on content creation, marketing strategies, and community engagement. Our goal is to help you succeed on your terms, without taking a huge chunk of your earnings. We only ask for a minimal percentage of your future winnings, and our contract terms are flexible and fair."

Jamie's sincerity was evident in his tone. "I understand that this offer might seem less flashy compared to what Victor is proposing. We don't have the same resources or reach, but we're passionate about helping emerging talents like you. Our focus is on creating a supportive environment where you can thrive without feeling overwhelmed by high demands."

As Jamie spoke, Alex felt a growing sense of comfort. The offer was modest but came with a personal touch that resonated with him. Jamie's enthusiasm and genuine interest in Alex's career were compelling. The thought of having someone who truly cared about his development, rather than a corporate entity driven by profits, was appealing.

"I appreciate the personal approach, Jamie," Alex said, his voice reflecting his genuine interest. "It's clear you're committed to helping me grow. Can you tell me more about how you plan to support me in terms of marketing and community building?"

Jamie's eyes lit up. "Absolutely. We'll work together to craft a content strategy that showcases your unique style and skills. We'll also help you engage with your audience through social media, live streams, and collaborations with other gamers. Our goal is to build a community around your brand and ensure that your growth is sustainable."

Alex took a moment to process everything. Jamie's offer was appealing not only for its fairness but also for the promise of a supportive partnership. The idea of building his career with someone who genuinely cared about his success was a stark contrast to the high-pressure environment Victor's offer implied.

"Thanks for explaining everything, Jamie," Alex said thoughtfully. "I'll need to weigh both offers carefully, but I really appreciate your transparency and support."

Jamie smiled warmly. "Take your time, Alex. If you have any questions or need more information, feel free to reach out. We're here to help you make the best decision for your future."

As the call ended, Alex sat back in his chair, feeling a sense of clarity about what mattered most to him. The choice between Victor and Jamie was not just about the immediate benefits but also about aligning his career with his personal values and long-term goals.

With both offers in hand, Alex knew he had a significant decision to make. The allure of Victor's high-profile offer was tempting, but Jamie's supportive and fair approach provided a compelling alternative. Alex was beginning to realize that the right choice would be about more than just financial gain—it would be about building a career that was both successful and true to who he was.

Chapter 3: The Pressure Builds

As Alex sat in his dimly lit room, the weight of his decision felt heavier than ever. The screen of his laptop displayed side-by-side notes on Victor Kline's and Jamie Ruiz's offers, a constant reminder of the crossroads he faced. He toggled between his gaming interface and the documents, trying to focus on his gameplay, but his thoughts kept drifting to the implications of each offer.

Victor Kline's proposal was undeniably tempting. The prospect of immediate fame and access to top-tier equipment was alluring. With Victor's backing, Alex could potentially skyrocket to prominence, joining the ranks of elite gamers and earning substantial rewards. The idea of participating in high-profile tournaments and gaining exposure to a vast audience was thrilling. However, the trade-off was significant—Victor's demand for a large percentage of Alex's future earnings and winnings was a substantial cost to consider.

On the other hand, Jamie Ruiz's offer was less glamorous but equally compelling in its own way. Jamie promised a supportive and personal approach, focusing on building Alex's career from the ground up. The minimal cut of Alex's earnings and the promise of hands-on guidance made Jamie's offer appealing. The idea of working closely with someone who genuinely cared about Alex's success and well-being was comforting. Yet, Jamie's limited influence and resources meant fewer immediate opportunities compared to what Victor could provide.

Alex leaned back in his chair, running a hand through his hair. The decision wasn't just about the financial aspects or the immediate benefits. It was about what kind of career he wanted to build and what kind of person he wanted to become. Did he want to chase after instant fame at the cost of his independence, or did he prefer to take a slower, more controlled path with someone who offered genuine support?

He thought about the long-term impact of each choice. Partnering with Victor might offer rapid success but at the risk of being tied to a contract that could limit his future freedom. The idea of being controlled by someone else's agenda was unsettling. In contrast, Jamie's offer, though less lucrative in the short term, promised a more sustainable and fulfilling career. Alex envisioned himself growing as a player and as a person, supported by someone who valued his individual journey.

The internal struggle intensified as Alex considered the opinions of those around him. His friends and family had shared their thoughts, each offering a perspective that added to the complexity of his decision. His best friend, Jake, was enthusiastic about the potential of working with Victor, citing the advantages of rapid success and increased visibility. Conversely, his older sister, Lisa, emphasized the importance of maintaining personal integrity and the value of a supportive partnership over the lure of immediate fame.

Alex's thoughts were interrupted by a notification from his phone. It was a message from Jamie, checking in to see if Alex had any more questions. The timing was both helpful and haunting, a reminder of the decision he still had to make. He appreciated Jamie's patience and the genuine concern evident in the message. It made Alex question whether the allure of Victor's offer was overshadowing what truly mattered.

With a sigh, Alex returned to his notes, meticulously comparing the pros and cons. He listed out his priorities—career growth, personal values, and long-term sustainability. The more he reflected, the more he realized that his choice needed to align with his values and aspirations, not just the immediate rewards.

As the night wore on, Alex found himself more uncertain than ever. The decision would define his future and shape his career in ways he couldn't yet fully understand. The pressure to make the right choice was overwhelming, and the fear of making a mistake was palpable.

He decided to take a break from his deliberations and clear his mind. Stepping away from his computer, Alex went for a walk around his neighborhood. The cool night air and the quiet streets provided a welcome respite from his thoughts. As he walked, he contemplated the bigger picture, hoping to gain some clarity on what path would ultimately bring him the fulfillment and success he sought.

The night's solitude offered a chance to reflect on what truly mattered to him. He realized that while both offers had their merits, his decision needed to align with his long-term vision for his career and his personal integrity. The path forward would be challenging, but it had to be one that he could stand behind wholeheartedly.

The pressure on Alex intensified as he began seeking advice from friends and family, each offering their own perspective on the dilemma he faced. The feedback he received was a mix of support, skepticism, and confusion, reflecting the complexity of his decision.

His best friend, Jake, was enthusiastic about Victor Kline's offer. "This is a once-in-a-lifetime chance, Alex," Jake said, his eyes wide with excitement. "Victor's connections could get you into the big leagues fast. Just think about all the exposure and opportunities you'd get. It's a huge risk, but it could pay off big time!" Jake's enthusiasm was palpable, and it was clear he was excited about the prospect of Alex becoming a top-tier gamer. But Alex couldn't shake the nagging feeling that Jake's excitement was more about the potential fame and less about the long-term implications.

In contrast, Alex's older sister, Lisa, took a more measured approach. "Look, I get that Victor's offer is tempting," she said, her voice calm but firm. "But you need to think about what's important to you. Jamie's offer might not seem as glamorous, but it's fair. You'd be working with someone who genuinely cares about your success and isn't trying to take a huge chunk of your earnings. Sometimes, it's better to build something solid from the ground up, even if it takes longer." Lisa's advice was thoughtful and grounded, emphasizing the importance of integrity and long-term growth over immediate rewards.

Alex also reached out to his gaming community, seeking opinions from fellow gamers and online friends. The responses were mixed. Some argued that partnering with Victor was a strategic move that could catapult Alex's career, while others echoed Lisa's sentiment, urging him to prioritize fairness and personal values. The range of opinions only added to Alex's confusion, as he struggled to balance the immediate benefits of fame with the ethical considerations of each offer.

One evening, as Alex sat down for dinner with his family, the topic of his decision came up. His parents, who had always been supportive but cautious, expressed their concerns. "We want what's best for you, Alex," his father said, looking at him with a mixture of pride and worry. "But you need to be careful. A deal with Victor could look great on paper, but it's important to understand the long-term consequences. We're here to support you, no matter what you decide, but make sure you think it through."

His mother, her voice tinged with concern, added, "And remember, no matter which path you choose, don't lose sight of who you are. It's easy to get caught up in the excitement, but staying true to yourself and your values is what really matters."

The conversation with his family was a sobering reminder of the stakes involved. Alex appreciated their support and advice, but the decision still felt overwhelming. Each perspective highlighted different aspects of his dilemma, making it difficult to arrive at a clear conclusion.

As the days went by, the weight of the decision grew heavier. Alex continued to analyze the pros and cons, weighing the advice he received against his own desires and goals. He spent sleepless nights considering the future, trying to envision what his life would be like under each scenario. The pressure to make the right choice was intense, and the fear of making a mistake loomed large.

The turning point came when Alex decided to take a step back from the constant analysis and seek some clarity. He scheduled a final meeting with both Victor and Jamie, hoping that direct conversations would provide the insight he needed. The meetings would give him an opportunity to ask questions, clarify terms, and perhaps gain a clearer sense of what each partnership would truly entail.

As Alex prepared for these meetings, he knew that the decision he faced was not just about choosing between two offers but about defining his future and aligning his career with his personal values. The advice from his friends and family had added layers of complexity to his decision, but it had also underscored the importance of making a choice that was true to who he was and what he wanted to achieve.

With determination and a sense of purpose, Alex geared up for the next phase of his journey, ready to confront the final details of each offer and ultimately make a decision that would shape his path forward.

Chapter 4: The Cost Of Fame

As Alex's success in "Battalion Blitz" continued to soar, the allure of Victor Kline's offer grew stronger. Each tournament and competitive match added to Alex's reputation as a formidable player, and with every victory, the prospect of partnering with Victor seemed increasingly tantalizing.

Alex's recent performance in the regional finals had been exceptional. His strategic gameplay and quick reflexes had earned him accolades from both fans and commentators. The buzz surrounding his name was palpable, and it was clear that his skills were garnering significant attention within the gaming community. It was during this period of heightened visibility that Victor Kline's influence became even more apparent.

Victor, a towering figure in the gaming industry, had a reputation for catapulting players to fame. His track record was impressive—numerous gamers had risen to stardom under his wing, and his endorsement carried immense weight. As Alex's profile grew, so did the temptation to accept Victor's high-profile offer.

In the midst of this success, Victor made another appearance, this time with an even more enticing proposal. He promised not only enhanced streaming equipment but also exclusive sponsorships and endorsements. The potential for Alex to become a household name in the gaming world was now within reach, thanks to Victor's connections and resources. The promise of a substantial increase in exposure and financial gain was hard to ignore.

Alex found himself torn between the excitement of these opportunities and the reality of the demands Victor was placing on him.

The prospect of fame was alluring, but it came with a cost. Victor's high percentage cut of Alex's future earnings, though substantial, seemed to be a trade-off for the immense benefits he offered. The lure of immediate success and recognition was compelling, especially in contrast to Jamie Ruiz's more modest but supportive offer.

The pressure to make the right decision was compounded by the visible success Alex was experiencing. His social media following was growing rapidly, and the competitive scene was buzzing with excitement about his potential. The idea of partnering with Victor, who could amplify this success and provide unparalleled opportunities, was increasingly tempting. The fear of missing out on this chance to make a significant leap in his career was a constant source of anxiety for Alex.

Late one evening, Alex sat in his room, staring at the glowing screen of his gaming setup. The lights of the gaming rig seemed to mock him with their promise of success. He reviewed Victor's latest offer again, contemplating the potential benefits and the steep price attached. The excitement of becoming a recognized name in the gaming world was powerful, but so was the nagging concern about the long-term implications of the high percentage Victor demanded.

As he pondered his decision, Alex couldn't help but reflect on the conversations he'd had with his friends and family. Each piece of advice seemed to echo in his mind, adding to the complexity of his choice. The allure of Victor's offer was undeniable, but it was also clear that accepting it would mean compromising a significant portion of his earnings and future autonomy.

The more successful Alex became, the more Victor's offer seemed to align with the dream he had always envisioned. The chance to work with a renowned figure and gain access to top-tier resources was a rare opportunity. Yet, amidst the glittering prospects, Alex remained haunted by the thought of losing control over his own career and the values he held dear.

As the days passed and the pressure mounted, Alex knew he needed to confront this decision head-on. The choice between Victor's high-stakes offer and Jamie's supportive partnership had never felt more critical. Each option represented a different path, with its own set of rewards and sacrifices. Alex understood that the decision he made would not only impact his career but also shape his future and personal values.

With the weight of this realization, Alex prepared himself for the final meetings with Victor and Jamie. He knew that he needed to approach these conversations with clarity and resolve, ready to make a choice that would define his path forward. The journey to the final level of his career had reached a pivotal moment, and Alex was determined to navigate it with both ambition and integrity.

As Alex's competitive success continued to make waves, the magnitude of Victor Kline's offer started to loom larger in his mind. Victor's latest pitch had included promises of not just advanced equipment and top-tier sponsorships, but also significant media exposure and exclusive access to high-profile events. The promise of a meteoric rise in his gaming career was incredibly enticing, and the prospect of fame seemed almost within reach.

However, the more Alex reflected on the offer, the more he began to question the cost. Victor's demands for a substantial percentage of Alex's future earnings and winnings weighed heavily on his conscience. Despite the immediate allure of fame and financial gain, Alex couldn't shake the feeling that agreeing to such a high percentage might jeopardize his long-term financial stability and career autonomy.

Sitting alone in his room, Alex reviewed the terms of Victor's offer once more. The figures and percentages seemed to blur together, but the stark reality of what he would be giving up became clearer with each passing minute. Victor's cut would leave Alex with a significantly reduced share of his earnings—money that he had worked tirelessly to earn through his skills and dedication. The thought of handing over such a substantial portion of his success to someone else was increasingly unsettling.

The stakes seemed to get higher with every tournament Alex competed in. His victories brought him closer to the top of the leaderboards, and with each success, Victor's influence grew more apparent. The prospect of becoming a high-profile gamer was thrilling, but Alex began to wonder if the price was too steep. He could almost hear Victor's voice promising the moon, but the cost attached to that promise began to feel overwhelming.

In conversations with his friends and family, Alex found himself expressing more concerns about Victor's offer. They could see the appeal of working with such a well-known figure, but they also shared Alex's apprehension about the percentage Victor demanded. Many of them voiced their worry that Alex might be sacrificing too much for a chance at quick success.

His father, who had always supported Alex's gaming ambitions despite the financial struggles, was particularly vocal. "I've seen you work so hard, Alex. Don't let someone take away what you've earned. You deserve to reap the rewards of your talent."

Alex's mother, though less involved in the gaming world, was equally concerned. "You've always been so dedicated. I just don't want you to give away too much of what you've worked for. You need to think about the long-term."

The more Alex listened to their concerns, the more he started to question whether the immediate benefits of Victor's offer were worth the long-term trade-offs. The financial and professional control he would be relinquishing weighed heavily on his mind. Despite the undeniable allure of Victor's offer, the prospect of losing a significant portion of his earnings and having less control over his career became increasingly daunting.

He also began to consider the possibility of future disputes and conflicts that might arise from such an arrangement. Would the percentage demanded by Victor leave him vulnerable to exploitation or disagreements down the line? The thought of navigating a potentially strained relationship with Victor, who would have a significant stake in his success, added to his unease.

As Alex prepared for another major tournament, he couldn't escape the shadow of Victor's offer. The pressure to make a decision was mounting, and the stakes felt higher than ever. He was caught between the promise of rapid success and the fear of compromising his future. The decision was not just about choosing between two offers but also about determining the kind of career and life he wanted to build for himself.

With each passing day, Alex knew he had to confront this decision with clarity and resolve. The choice between Victor's high-stakes offer and Jamie's more modest but supportive partnership was becoming increasingly critical. As the day of the final meetings approached, Alex understood that he needed to weigh the immediate allure of fame against the long-term impact on his career and values.

Chapter 5: Building Trust

Alex's decision to consider Jamie Ruiz's offer more seriously brought about a shift in his focus. As the weeks progressed, he found himself increasingly interacting with Jamie, whose genuine passion and commitment to his success began to resonate deeply with him. Unlike the flashy promises of Victor Kline, Jamie's approach was grounded in authenticity and support.

Their meetings were more than just business discussions; they were opportunities for Alex to understand Jamie's vision for his career. Jamie took the time to learn about Alex's goals, not just as a gamer but as an individual with unique aspirations and challenges. These conversations helped Alex see Jamie's dedication to fostering his growth, rather than just capitalizing on his talent.

Jamie's support went beyond mere words. He provided Alex with practical help, including access to streaming equipment and resources that were crucial for improving Alex's online presence. More importantly, Jamie offered guidance on how to enhance his gameplay and manage his growing public profile. This mentorship was invaluable, as Alex had often felt isolated in his gaming journey due to a lack of professional support.

During one of their sessions, Jamie shared insights about building a brand and connecting with fans in a meaningful way. "It's not just about winning tournaments," Jamie explained. "It's about creating a community and maintaining a genuine connection with your audience. That's what will sustain your career in the long run."

Alex began to appreciate the value of Jamie's guidance. He realized that Jamie's offer wasn't just about financial terms but about creating a foundation for a successful and sustainable career. Jamie's focus on long-term growth rather than immediate gains started to align with Alex's own values and aspirations.

As Alex continued to work with Jamie, he started to see tangible improvements in his gameplay and online presence. His streaming quality improved, and his audience grew more engaged with his content. The support and advice from Jamie were clearly making a difference, and Alex's confidence began to build.

Jamie's approach also helped Alex navigate the complexities of the gaming industry. He provided practical advice on dealing with sponsors, managing social media, and balancing personal life with professional commitments. This holistic support was something Alex had been missing and was beginning to realize its importance.

The more Alex worked with Jamie, the more he felt a sense of partnership and trust. Jamie's dedication to his success, coupled with the practical assistance he provided, was creating a positive impact on Alex's career. This new perspective helped Alex see the true value of Jamie's offer and the potential for a successful partnership built on mutual respect and support.

With each passing day, Alex's decision to explore Jamie's offer seemed more justified. The tangible benefits of Jamie's mentorship and the genuine support he provided began to overshadow the immediate allure of Victor's high-profile offer. Alex was increasingly convinced that Jamie's approach would help him build a more sustainable and fulfilling career in gaming.

As Alex settled into his partnership with Jamie Ruiz, the benefits of the supportive mentorship became increasingly evident. Jamie's guidance was not only practical but also instrumental in Alex's development, both as a gamer and as an individual. This phase of Alex's journey was marked by small victories that, together, built a solid foundation for his future success.

One of the first noticeable improvements came with Alex's gameplay. Jamie's advice on refining strategies and mastering new techniques led to a series of impressive performances in online tournaments. Alex's skill set expanded, and his gameplay became more sophisticated and nuanced. His ability to analyze opponents and adapt to various game scenarios improved significantly, which was reflected in his rising rankings and accolades.

Beyond the gameplay, Jamie's focus on Alex's streaming presence also yielded positive results. Jamie helped Alex set up a professional streaming environment, enhancing the visual and audio quality of his broadcasts. With Jamie's help, Alex began to craft a more engaging and interactive experience for his viewers. He learned to manage live chats effectively, create compelling content, and maintain a consistent online presence. This professional polish not only attracted more viewers but also fostered a stronger connection with his audience.

One particularly memorable moment came during a mid-level tournament where Alex, using strategies Jamie had suggested, executed a flawless game plan that led his team to victory. This win, while not a major championship, was a testament to the progress he had made under Jamie's mentorship. The victory was celebrated not just as a personal achievement but as a significant step in the right direction for Alex's career.

Jamie also emphasized the importance of maintaining balance and well-being. He encouraged Alex to take breaks, manage stress, and focus on personal development alongside gaming. This holistic approach helped Alex stay grounded and avoid burnout, a common issue among competitive gamers. Jamie's mentorship extended beyond gaming strategies, offering advice on managing time, setting goals, and maintaining a healthy lifestyle.

Alex's growth was also evident in his interactions with other players and fans. Jamie's lessons on building a brand and engaging with the community helped Alex develop a more authentic and relatable persona.

He became known not just for his skills but also for his positive attitude and genuine interactions with his audience. This reputation helped him build a loyal fanbase and attract potential sponsors, further establishing his place in the gaming community.

As Alex reflected on his progress, he felt a deep sense of gratitude for Jamie's support. The growth he experienced was not just about winning games but about evolving as a professional and as a person. Jamie's mentorship had provided him with the tools and insights needed to navigate the complexities of the gaming world, and the positive results were clear in both his performance and his personal development.

The small victories and incremental growth under Jamie's guidance were proving to be a powerful testament to the value of a supportive and genuine partnership. Alex's decision to choose Jamie over Victor Kline's high-profile offer was increasingly validated by the tangible progress and the meaningful relationships he was building. As he continued on this path, Alex was more convinced than ever that Jamie's mentorship was the key to achieving his long-term goals and creating a fulfilling career in gaming.

Chapter 6: Tournament Trials

The excitement in the gaming community was palpable as the major "Battalion Blitz" tournament approached. For Alex Carter, this was more than just another competition; it was a critical moment that would test his skills, determination, and the value of his recent decisions. With both Victor Kline and Jamie Ruiz involved in his career, the stakes had never been higher.

The tournament was set to be one of the most prestigious in the gaming calendar, attracting top players from around the world. Alex knew that performing well here could significantly impact his future. He spent the weeks leading up to the event refining his strategies, practicing relentlessly, and preparing himself mentally. The weight of expectation was immense, not just from his fans but also from Victor and Jamie, each with their own vested interests in his success.

Victor Kline, who had initially promised access to top-notch resources and exposure, had been somewhat distant since Alex's decision to partner with Jamie. The high-profile figure's support now felt more like a distant promise than an active contribution. However, Victor's reputation loomed large, and Alex couldn't help but feel the pressure of the potential fallout if things didn't go well.

On the other hand, Jamie Ruiz had been a constant source of encouragement and practical support. Jamie had provided Alex with advanced training tools, offered strategic advice, and helped him with the logistics of tournament preparation. Jamie's presence was a reassuring constant, emphasizing the value of a partnership grounded in genuine support rather than mere transactional interests.

As the tournament commenced, Alex's performance was under intense scrutiny. Each match brought its own set of challenges, and the competition was fierce. Alex's gameplay was a mix of calculated risks and daring maneuvers, a testament to the strategies Jamie had helped him develop. He found himself facing opponents who had been preparing for this event just as diligently, making every victory hard-earned.

The pressure mounted with each round, and Alex's team advanced through the brackets, facing tougher and tougher rivals. The support from Jamie proved invaluable during these critical moments. Jamie was in constant contact, providing real-time advice and encouragement that kept Alex focused and motivated. Unlike Victor's distant involvement, Jamie's hands-on approach was a stark contrast, and it became increasingly clear how much of an asset this partnership was.

Alex's performance in the tournament became a balancing act between showcasing his skills and managing the expectations that came with both Victor's and Jamie's support. The strain of competing at such a high level was palpable, but Alex's confidence was bolstered by the consistent backing of Jamie's mentorship.

As the tournament reached its climax, Alex's team was on the brink of securing a top spot. The final rounds were intense, with every match requiring peak performance and strategic finesse. Alex knew that the outcome of this tournament would not only impact his ranking but also reflect on the value of his choices in managing his career. The pressure to deliver was immense, and the contrasting nature of Victor's and Jamie's support became more apparent than ever.

The final rounds of the "Battalion Blitz" tournament were a whirlwind of adrenaline and strategy. As the competition reached its zenith, the tension in the gaming arena was almost palpable. Alex's performance had been exceptional, demonstrating both his skill and the effectiveness of Jamie's guidance. Each victory brought him closer to the top prize, but also heightened the scrutiny of his choices.

The final match was the ultimate test. Alex faced off against the reigning champion, a player known for their aggressive style and unyielding tactics. The match was intense, with both players pushing their limits. Alex's team managed to gain a slight edge, but the outcome was still uncertain until the last few moments. The crowd was on the edge of their seats, and the pressure on Alex was immense.

As the final match concluded, Alex emerged victorious. The victory was celebrated with cheers and applause, but it was accompanied by a flurry of media attention and social media buzz. The win had catapulted him to new heights of recognition, and he was inundated with congratulations from fans, fellow gamers, and industry insiders.

In the aftermath of the tournament, the results brought Alex face-to-face with the consequences of his decisions. The media coverage highlighted both his success and the contrasting nature of his partnerships. Victor Kline's absence was noticeable; while Victor had promised exposure and high-profile connections, his involvement had been limited to a distant endorsement. The lack of direct support from Victor during the tournament was starkly evident.

Conversely, Jamie Ruiz's presence was a constant throughout the tournament. Jamie had been there at every critical moment, offering real-time advice, emotional support, and practical assistance. The difference in support was clear, and Alex found himself reflecting on what mattered most to him in his career.

The victory was a significant milestone, but it came with a moment of introspection. Alex was faced with the realization that while Victor's high-profile offer had the potential for immediate rewards, it lacked the genuine support and personal connection that Jamie had provided. Jamie's involvement had proven to be invaluable, not just in terms of practical help but in fostering an environment where Alex could thrive on his own terms.

Alex began to question whether the glamour of Victor's offer was worth the trade-off of personal integrity and authentic support. The tournament results forced him to re-evaluate his priorities, considering what kind of career he wanted to build and what values he wanted to uphold. The success he had achieved with Jamie's support made it clear that the sustainable growth and genuine partnership mattered more to him than the fleeting allure of high-profile endorsements.

As Alex reflected on his experiences, he felt a renewed sense of clarity about his future. The tournament had not only showcased his skills but also highlighted the importance of choosing a path that aligned with his personal values and long-term goals. The decision he had made to partner with Jamie was increasingly reaffirmed, and Alex was more determined than ever to build his career on a foundation of trust, support, and authenticity.

Chapter 7: The Turning Point

The day after his triumphant victory at the "Battalion Blitz" tournament, Alex Carter found himself grappling with an unexpected personal crisis. While the buzz of his win should have been exhilarating, a troubling phone call from home cast a shadow over his celebration. His mother had been in a minor car accident, and although she was not seriously injured, the situation required immediate attention.

Alex's focus shifted abruptly from gaming to family concerns. The accident, while not life-threatening, stirred a deep sense of anxiety and responsibility in him. With his mother needing time to recover and his father unable to take time off work, Alex was thrust into the role of caregiver for his younger siblings. The shift in his responsibilities was jarring, pulling him away from the game and the spotlight he had recently enjoyed.

As Alex balanced his new duties with his gaming commitments, the stress began to impact his performance. His concentration faltered, and he found it challenging to maintain the same level of dedication he had previously shown. The personal crisis, combined with the pressure of living up to his recent success, started to weigh heavily on him. The once-clear path to his gaming career was now clouded with uncertainty and fatigue.

During this period, Jamie Ruiz proved to be an anchor of support. Understanding the gravity of Alex's situation, Jamie offered not only practical advice but also emotional encouragement. He reassured Alex that his family responsibilities were important and that taking time to address them was both valid and necessary. Jamie's empathy and flexibility allowed Alex to take a step back and focus on his family without the added pressure of professional obligations.

Despite Jamie's support, Alex struggled internally. The disruption to his gaming routine and the emotional toll of his personal crisis made him question his ability to handle both his responsibilities at home and his ambitions in the gaming world. He faced sleepless nights, juggling schoolwork, caregiving, and attempts to maintain his gaming skills.

This period of reflection and struggle brought Alex to a critical juncture. The crisis forced him to evaluate what truly mattered to him—his career aspirations or his family responsibilities. It also highlighted the contrasting nature of his two offers. While Victor Kline's high-profile support seemed enticing, it lacked the personal connection that Jamie provided. In contrast, Jamie's support was rooted in understanding and genuine care, offering a sense of stability during Alex's turbulent time.

As Alex navigated through this personal crisis, he began to see the value in having a supportive and understanding partner. Jamie's consistent support during his most challenging moments reinforced the importance of choosing a path aligned with his values and personal needs. The turning point was not just about making a career decision but also about recognizing the kind of professional and personal relationships that would truly support his long-term growth and well-being.

The weeks following the accident were filled with a whirlwind of adjustments for Alex. Managing his new responsibilities at home while trying to maintain his gaming performance proved to be an exhausting balancing act. As his mother recovered, the burden of caregiving for his siblings and managing household chores weighed heavily on him. Yet, through it all, Jamie Ruiz remained a steadfast source of support.

Jamie's support was more than just occasional check-ins or words of encouragement. He reached out regularly to see how Alex was managing both his family and gaming commitments. On top of that, Jamie offered practical solutions, such as adjusting Alex's schedule for gaming practice and providing access to resources that could help him manage his time more effectively.

One day, Jamie surprised Alex with a video call. He was holding up a package, which he promptly opened to reveal a high-quality gaming headset and a portable streaming setup. "I know things have been rough lately," Jamie said, his voice filled with empathy. "I figured this might help you manage your streams a bit better without having to worry about your equipment failing."

Alex was taken aback by the gesture. The new equipment would make a significant difference in his gaming setup and reduce some of the stress he was under. It was not just the material support that struck him but the thoughtfulness behind it. Jamie's actions demonstrated a level of understanding and commitment that went beyond business. It was a genuine investment in Alex's well-being and future.

As Alex adjusted to his new equipment and incorporated it into his routine, he began to notice subtle improvements in his gameplay. The enhanced setup made streaming smoother, and the lessening technical issues allowed him to focus more on his strategy and performance. The small victories started to reappear, boosting his confidence and reminding him of his potential.

Jamie's consistent presence during this challenging time gave Alex a renewed sense of stability. Whenever Alex felt overwhelmed, he could count on Jamie to offer practical advice and emotional support. This unwavering support helped Alex rediscover his passion for gaming and rekindled his motivation to succeed.

Reflecting on the past few months, Alex began to recognize the profound impact Jamie's support had on him. Jamie had become more than a manager; he was a mentor who genuinely cared about Alex's personal and professional growth. This realization was a crucial turning point for Alex as he weighed his future in the gaming industry.

The contrast between Jamie's support and the pressure from Victor Kline became increasingly clear. While Victor's offer was tempting with its promise of fame and resources, it lacked the personal touch and understanding that Jamie provided. Jamie's support was a reminder that success wasn't just about financial gains or high-profile endorsements but also about the relationships and values that shaped one's journey.

As Alex faced this critical juncture, he felt a growing certainty that the choice he needed to make was not just about professional advancement but about aligning his career with his values and the support that had been crucial during his most trying times. Jamie's unwavering support had not only helped him through a personal crisis but had also reinforced the importance of choosing a path that resonated with his integrity and long-term vision.

Chapter 8: The Dilemma Intensifies

As Alex continued to gain recognition in "Battalion Blitz," the stakes of his decision grew increasingly complex. His performance in recent tournaments had catapulted him into the spotlight, and with every victory, his fame and potential earnings expanded. This newfound success attracted the attention of more sponsors and media outlets, further heightening the pressure on Alex to make a choice about his future.

Victor Kline, having noticed Alex's rising prominence, intensified his efforts to sway Alex toward his offer. The high-profile figure started making frequent contact, emphasizing how the growing media buzz and sponsorship opportunities were perfect for leveraging his offer. Victor's messages and calls were increasingly urgent, laden with promises of exclusive deals, top-tier streaming setups, and a rapid ascent to the pinnacle of gaming fame.

One evening, as Alex was winding down after a grueling practice session, his phone rang. It was Victor. "Alex, I've been watching your matches. You're on fire, and this is the moment to capitalize on it," Victor said, his voice filled with a sense of urgency. "If you're serious about taking your career to the next level, you need to make a move now. The longer you wait, the more opportunities you might miss."

Victor outlined a new, more enticing aspect of his offer: a partnership with a major gaming brand that would significantly boost Alex's exposure. "This is not just about the present," Victor continued. "Think about the future. With this deal, you could be a household name. You'll have access to the best training facilities, top-tier equipment, and a network that can take you further than you ever imagined."

The offer sounded more tempting than ever, and Alex could feel the pull of the possibility of instant fame and success. However, the increased urgency of Victor's pitch also brought with it an undeniable pressure. The prospect of missing out on such a lucrative opportunity if he didn't act quickly added to his stress and uncertainty.

In contrast, Jamie Ruiz's approach remained steady and consistent. Despite the growing allure of Victor's high-profile offer, Jamie continued to support Alex with unwavering dedication. Jamie's communications were always supportive, focusing on Alex's long-term growth and well-being rather than immediate fame. He provided practical advice on managing his rising success and reassured Alex that he was still committed to helping him achieve his goals, regardless of the challenges.

One afternoon, while Alex was contemplating Victor's latest proposal, Jamie reached out with a simple but profound message: "Alex, remember why you started. It's not just about reaching the top—it's about how you get there and who you become along the way. I'm here to support you, no matter the path you choose."

The contrast between the two offers became increasingly stark. Victor's approach was flashy and promising immediate rewards, but it came with strings attached that could jeopardize Alex's autonomy and integrity. Jamie's support, while less glamorous, was grounded in a genuine commitment to Alex's growth and values.

As Alex weighed the implications of Victor's urgent pitch against Jamie's steadfast support, he found himself at a crossroads. The pressure to choose between the immediate allure of Victor's offer and the sustainable, value-driven support from Jamie was mounting, intensifying the dilemma he faced.

The pressure was mounting as Alex approached the final round of a major gaming tournament. This tournament wasn't just a test of his skills; it was a critical juncture that could influence his decision between Victor Kline and Jamie Ruiz. The competition was fierce, and Alex's performance would be scrutinized by both potential partners, each watching closely to gauge his potential.

Alex sat alone in his room, his gaming setup glowing softly in the dim light. He reviewed his notes and strategies, but his mind kept drifting to the decision he faced. The excitement of the tournament was overshadowed by the looming choice that would shape his future.

Victor's recent messages had become more insistent. He was pushing for a decision, stressing that the window for the gaming brand partnership was closing. "You're at the top now, Alex. Make the right choice, and you'll be set for life," Victor's last message had read. The offer was more enticing than ever, with promises of instant fame and a high-profile network.

On the other hand, Jamie's support remained constant and steady. He had been a pillar of encouragement, always ready with practical advice and unwavering belief in Alex's potential. Jamie's messages were full of encouragement, focusing on Alex's personal growth and long-term success. "Play your game, Alex. Focus on what you love and let that guide you," Jamie had said before the tournament.

The night before the final round, Alex's room was filled with a tense silence. He lay in bed, staring at the ceiling, his thoughts tangled in a web of anxiety and uncertainty. His family, still struggling financially, had shown pride in his achievements but was also anxious about the implications of the decision. They trusted Alex to make the best choice but worried about the long-term impact of either option.

The next day, Alex entered the tournament arena with a heavy heart. His team was relying on him, and the stakes felt higher than ever. The noise of the crowd, the flashing lights, and the pressure of the competition combined to create a whirlwind of emotions.

As the tournament progressed, Alex played with remarkable skill and focus, but he couldn't shake the weight of his decision. With each round, he became more aware of how his choice could affect not just his career but also his sense of self and values.

During a break between matches, Alex stepped outside for some fresh air. He leaned against the wall, his thoughts racing. He considered Victor's offer and the promises of immediate success, but also the potential cost of losing control over his career. He contrasted this with Jamie's unwavering support, which, while less glamorous, offered a more personal and sustainable path.

In that moment of reflection, Alex realized the decision wasn't just about the financial aspects or immediate gains. It was about aligning his career with his personal values and long-term goals. He knew that the choice between Victor and Jamie was not just a business decision but a reflection of what kind of professional—and person—he wanted to be.

The final match approached, and Alex had to clear his mind and focus on the game. As he sat down at his console, he resolved to make the decision that would not only shape his career but also honor his own principles. The outcome of the tournament might influence the offer on the table, but it was clear that his choice would define his path beyond the game.

Alex took a deep breath and immersed himself in the game, determined to give his best performance. Regardless of the outcome, he knew that the choice he would make in the coming days would be pivotal, and he needed to be prepared for whatever lay ahead.

Chapter 9: The Breaking Point

The morning after the final match of the tournament, Alex woke up to a mix of anticipation and dread. The days leading up to this moment had been filled with intense focus and stress, but now the moment of decision was at hand. With the tournament behind him, the offers from Victor Kline and Jamie Ruiz were no longer just abstract possibilities—they were real and immediate.

Alex's room was cluttered with notes, messages, and reminders of the decision he had to make. Victor's offers had been increasingly aggressive, highlighting the potential for immediate success but emphasizing the high price Alex would pay in terms of earnings and control. Jamie's approach had been steady and supportive, with a focus on long-term growth and fair terms.

As he reviewed the details of each offer one last time, Alex could almost hear Victor's voice, with its promise of fame and recognition. Victor had sent one final message, expressing urgency and the need for a quick response: "This is your chance to secure a future, Alex. Don't let it slip away."

Jamie's messages had been less frequent but more heartfelt. Jamie's last note was a reminder of what had always been at the core of their discussions: "Your talent deserves to shine, and it will. But it has to be on your terms. I believe in you."

Alex had spent countless nights weighing the pros and cons, talking to his family, and even seeking advice from friends. The financial implications, the potential for fame, and the values he held close all played into his decision. His family had been supportive but had also left the final choice up to him, knowing that whatever he decided would have a significant impact on his future.

Sitting at his desk, Alex took a deep breath and considered the future. He thought about his experiences with both Victor and Jamie. Victor's promises were enticing but came with strings attached. The potential for immediate success was undeniable, but Alex felt uneasy about the percentage of his earnings he would lose and the loss of creative control.

Jamie's support had been a constant source of stability. The offer was modest compared to Victor's, but it was genuine and fair. Jamie had shown him the importance of building a career on his own terms, fostering real connections, and growing at a pace that respected his values.

The decision made, Alex composed a response to Victor. He thanked him for the opportunity but explained that he had chosen to pursue a different path that aligned better with his personal values and long-term goals.

With his decision made, Alex then sent a message to Jamie, accepting the offer and expressing his excitement to work together. He was ready to commit to a partnership that promised to be supportive and respectful of his aspirations.

As he hit the send button on both messages, Alex felt a wave of relief mixed with apprehension. The choice had been difficult, but he knew it was the right one for him. Now, it was time to face the consequences of his decision and deal with the immediate fallout.

The days that followed were a whirlwind. Victor's reaction was swift and harsh. He publicly announced his disappointment in a social media post, painting Alex's decision as a missed opportunity and suggesting that Alex was not serious about his career. The post drew a lot of attention, and Alex faced a flurry of questions and speculation from fans and the gaming community.

On the other hand, Jamie's response was supportive and positive. He welcomed Alex into the partnership with enthusiasm and began planning ways to leverage the support and resources he could offer. Jamie's encouragement and strategic planning helped Alex navigate the backlash from Victor's public comments.

Alex's decision had set him on a path of its own, and he now had to deal with the implications. The gaming world was watching, and his choice was making waves. As he prepared to embark on this new chapter with Jamie, he knew that the road ahead would be challenging but also full of potential.

The decision was made, and Alex felt a mixture of relief and apprehension as he moved forward with Jamie Ruiz. However, the fallout from his choice was swift and dramatic. Victor Kline's public reaction had stirred up a storm in the gaming community, and Alex was now the center of intense scrutiny.

Victor's social media post not only criticized Alex's decision but also implied that Alex was ungrateful and uncommitted to his career. The gaming forums and news outlets quickly picked up the story, amplifying the backlash. Alex found himself bombarded with questions from fans, journalists, and even other gamers. The narrative that Alex had chosen to forsake a golden opportunity for a smaller, less influential offer began to take hold.

Amidst the chaos, Alex's phone was a constant flurry of notifications. Messages ranged from supportive words from friends and family to harsh criticisms from those who felt he had made a mistake. His social media accounts, once a source of pride, were now flooded with comments and opinions from people he didn't know personally.

Jamie, on the other hand, remained a steady presence throughout this turbulent time. He reached out to Alex with reassurance and practical advice. Jamie understood the industry's ebb and flow and knew how to navigate through such public scrutiny. He encouraged Alex to focus on what mattered most—their partnership and the long-term vision they had for Alex's career.

Despite Jamie's support, the immediate impact of Alex's decision on his relationships was palpable. Some of his closest friends, who had been vocal about the potential benefits of Victor's offer, began to distance themselves. They were disappointed or frustrated with Alex's choice, unable to see past the immediate financial and professional opportunities that Victor represented.

Alex's family, though initially worried, rallied behind him. They saw his choice as a brave step toward maintaining his values and integrity. Their support was a comforting anchor amid the storm, but even they could not shield him from the widespread negativity.

As Alex adjusted to his new partnership with Jamie, he had to confront the realities of his decision. The early days of the new arrangement were fraught with challenges. Jamie's support was instrumental, but the road to establishing credibility and making an impact was not smooth. Alex had to work harder than ever to prove that his choice was the right one.

In the competitive world of gaming, the immediate attention from Victor's fallout had consequences. Alex's performance in the subsequent tournaments was closely watched, and every move was analyzed with heightened scrutiny. The pressure to succeed was immense, and failure would only reinforce the critics' views.

Yet, through the turbulence, Alex began to see the value of his decision. Jamie's strategic guidance and authentic support were proving beneficial. Together, they focused on building Alex's brand, improving his skills, and creating content that resonated with his audience.

Despite the challenges, Alex remained resolute. He knew that his decision was not just about professional success but about staying true to his values. With Jamie's continued support and a renewed sense of purpose, Alex was determined to navigate the path he had chosen and ultimately prove that his choice was the right one for his long-term career and personal growth.

Chapter 10: New Beginnings

With his decision made and the whirlwind of the past few weeks slowly subsiding, Alex Carter settled into his new partnership with Jamie Ruiz. The immediate backlash had faded, and now, it was time to focus on the future. The shift from the high-profile pressure of Victor Kline to the more grounded support of Jamie was both challenging and refreshing.

Jamie's office, a modest space filled with gaming memorabilia and motivational posters, became Alex's new hub. It was a far cry from the glitz and glamour of Victor's world, but it was where Alex found his footing. Jamie's approach was hands-on and personal, offering Alex not just guidance but also practical tools and resources to enhance his streaming setup.

One of the first changes Alex noticed was the improvement in his equipment. Jamie had arranged for a state-of-the-art streaming setup, which included a high-quality microphone, a professional-grade camera, and upgraded gaming peripherals. The new gear made a significant difference in the quality of Alex's streams, and he could see the positive feedback from his growing audience.

Jamie also introduced Alex to a network of smaller but dedicated influencers and content creators. This new network might not have had the immediate clout of Victor's connections, but it provided Alex with genuine interactions and collaborations. Working with these creators helped Alex refine his content and expand his reach in a more authentic way.

The tournaments continued, but Alex approached them with a renewed sense of purpose. With Jamie's encouragement, he focused on honing his skills and developing strategies that played to his strengths. Jamie's mentorship included not only game tactics but also advice on managing stress and maintaining a balanced lifestyle.

As Alex's gameplay improved, so did his confidence. The steady support from Jamie and the better equipment contributed to a noticeable increase in his performance. He began to secure higher rankings and achieve personal bests in tournaments, which reflected positively on his streaming numbers and engagement with his audience.

One of the key benefits of Jamie's partnership was the emphasis on long-term growth rather than immediate fame. Jamie encouraged Alex to set realistic goals and build his brand steadily. They worked on creating a content schedule that included regular streams, engaging with fans through Q&A sessions, and producing informative and entertaining videos about gaming strategies and tips.

This methodical approach was different from the high-pressure environment Alex had experienced with Victor. It allowed him to grow at his own pace, and the results were beginning to show. Fans appreciated the authenticity and consistency Alex brought to his streams, which helped him build a loyal following.

In addition to his professional development, Alex noticed positive changes in his personal life. The support from Jamie and the stability of his new setup helped alleviate some of the stress he had been feeling. He reconnected with friends who had distanced themselves after his decision, and he found a renewed sense of balance in his life.

Alex's journey with Jamie was just beginning, but the early signs were promising. The new partnership was not without its challenges, but the benefits were becoming increasingly evident. With each passing day, Alex grew more confident in his decision, seeing the value in building his career on his own terms while staying true to his principles.

As weeks turned into months, Alex Carter's decision to partner with Jamie Ruiz began to show tangible results. The growth was not just in his gaming performance but also in his personal development, which was equally significant.

Alex's gaming skills continued to improve under Jamie's guidance. Jamie's approach to coaching was holistic, focusing on both strategic gameplay and mental fortitude. Alex learned advanced techniques and refined his strategies, but more importantly, he developed the ability to stay calm under pressure and to adapt quickly to the ever-changing dynamics of "Battalion Blitz."

The tournaments continued, and Alex's performances were consistently strong. His recent success in the "Legends Cup" was a testament to his hard work and Jamie's mentorship. Alex felt more confident than ever, and it showed in his gameplay. His streams garnered more viewers, and his engagement with fans became more personal and meaningful.

Outside the gaming world, Jamie's influence extended into Alex's personal life. Jamie encouraged Alex to maintain a healthy balance between his gaming career and other aspects of his life. They worked together to create a schedule that allowed Alex to spend time with friends and family, exercise regularly, and pursue other interests.

Alex took these lessons to heart. He began to manage his time better, making room for activities beyond gaming. This newfound balance helped him avoid burnout and kept his motivation high. He also reconnected with friends he had neglected during his intense focus on gaming, and these relationships provided him with a support system outside of the virtual world.

Jamie's impact was also evident in Alex's approach to challenges. With Jamie's encouragement, Alex learned to view setbacks as opportunities for growth rather than failures. This shift in mindset helped him navigate the ups and downs of his career with resilience and a positive outlook.

Moreover, Alex's interactions with the gaming community became more rewarding. Jamie's network of influencers and content creators provided Alex with opportunities to collaborate on projects that aligned with his interests. These collaborations not only expanded his reach but also allowed him to contribute to the community in meaningful ways.

One of the most significant changes was in Alex's approach to his fans. Jamie emphasized the importance of genuine engagement, and Alex took this advice to heart. He began to interact more with his viewers, responding to comments, hosting live Q&A sessions, and sharing behind-the-scenes glimpses of his life. This authenticity resonated with his audience and helped him build a loyal and supportive fan base.

Alex's growth as a gamer and as a person was evident in the way he handled the increasing demands of his career. He became more strategic in his approach, more mindful of his well-being, and more connected to his audience. Jamie's mentorship had not only improved his gameplay but also helped him develop the skills and mindset necessary for long-term success.

As Alex looked back on his journey, he felt a deep sense of gratitude for the decision he had made. Partnering with Jamie had provided him with the support and guidance he needed to thrive both professionally and personally. The benefits of this partnership were clear, and Alex was excited about the future and the new opportunities that lay ahead.

In this chapter of his life, Alex was not just growing as a gamer; he was evolving into a well-rounded individual who understood the value of balance, resilience, and genuine connections. The foundation Jamie had helped him build was strong, and Alex was ready to take on the next challenges with confidence and integrity.

Chapter 11: The Rewards of Integrity

As the months passed, Alex Carter's decision to partner with Jamie Ruiz began to yield remarkable results. The benefits of his choice were becoming increasingly clear, both in his professional gaming career and his personal life.

Alex's performance in "Battalion Blitz" had reached new heights. The strategies and techniques he had learned from Jamie paid off in tournaments and competitions. He had started to consistently place in the top ranks, earning recognition and respect within the gaming community. His gameplay was not only skillful but also showcased his unique style, which had developed into a signature trademark of his brand.

The partnership with Jamie had provided Alex with the tools and support he needed to excel. With access to better equipment and a structured training regimen, Alex was able to stream with high-quality visuals and sound, engaging his audience more effectively. His follower count grew steadily, and his streams became a regular destination for fans who appreciated his genuine personality and skillful play.

Beyond the technical improvements, Alex felt a deep sense of satisfaction in how he was achieving success. He was building his career on his own terms, without compromising his values or giving away a significant portion of his earnings. Jamie's fair and transparent approach ensured that Alex retained a substantial share of his winnings, allowing him to reinvest in his career and personal growth.

Alex's achievements were not limited to the gaming world. His increased visibility led to opportunities beyond gaming. He was invited to participate in panels and discussions about the gaming industry, where he shared his experiences and insights. These engagements helped him establish himself as a respected voice in the community, further enhancing his credibility and influence.

The personal growth Alex experienced was equally significant. The balance he had achieved in his life—between gaming, family, friends, and other interests—had contributed to his overall well-being. He no longer felt the strain of neglecting other aspects of his life for the sake of his career. Instead, he was thriving both professionally and personally, a testament to the wisdom of his decision to partner with Jamie.

As Alex continued to build on his success, he also remained committed to giving back to the community. Inspired by Jamie's mentorship and the support he had received, Alex began to mentor aspiring gamers himself. He used his platform to highlight emerging talent, share valuable tips, and promote a positive and supportive gaming culture.

Alex's journey was a clear demonstration of the rewards of integrity. By choosing a partnership that aligned with his values, he had achieved success on his own terms. His career was flourishing, and he was making a meaningful impact both in and out of the gaming world.

The pride Alex felt in his accomplishments was matched only by his gratitude for Jamie's unwavering support. The partnership had proven to be more than just a professional arrangement—it had become a cornerstone of Alex's growth and success. As he looked ahead, Alex was confident that the path he had chosen was not only the right one but also the most fulfilling.

As Alex continued to flourish in his gaming career, the bond between him and Jamie Ruiz grew stronger. Jamie's role went beyond that of a manager; he became a mentor, friend, and a pillar of support in Alex's life.

Jamie's dedication to Alex was evident in every aspect of their partnership. He was not just managing Alex's career but actively involved in his growth. Jamie regularly provided feedback on Alex's performance, both in tournaments and on his streams. Their discussions were not limited to gaming strategies but extended to personal development, ensuring that Alex remained grounded despite his rising fame.

The mentorship Jamie provided was invaluable. He helped Alex navigate the complexities of the gaming industry, offering guidance on handling media appearances, sponsorships, and community engagement. Jamie's approach was always centered on Alex's well-being and long-term success, rather than short-term gains.

Their relationship also became a source of inspiration for others. Alex began to use his platform to speak about the importance of having genuine support and mentorship in the competitive world of gaming. He frequently credited Jamie for his success, emphasizing how Jamie's fair and supportive partnership had made a significant difference in his career.

The impact of Jamie's support was most evident during challenging times. Whenever Alex faced setbacks or moments of self-doubt, Jamie was there to offer encouragement and practical advice. His presence provided Alex with the confidence to overcome obstacles and stay focused on his goals.

Moreover, the success Alex achieved under Jamie's mentorship allowed him to reinvest in the community. He set up a scholarship fund for aspiring gamers from underprivileged backgrounds, aiming to provide them with the resources and opportunities that had once been out of his reach. This initiative was a direct reflection of the values Jamie had instilled in him—emphasizing the importance of giving back and supporting others.

As Alex's career continued to grow, he and Jamie celebrated many milestones together. Their partnership was a testament to the power of trust, integrity, and genuine support. Jamie's role in Alex's life had evolved into something profound—an enduring friendship built on mutual respect and shared values.

In their conversations, Alex often reflected on how different his journey might have been if he had chosen Victor's offer. He recognized that while Victor's opportunity had been enticing, it would have come with significant compromises. The rewards of staying true to his principles and choosing Jamie had proven to be far more fulfilling.

The depth of Alex and Jamie's relationship became a cornerstone of Alex's success. It was clear that their partnership was not just about achieving professional goals but about building a legacy of integrity and support in the gaming community.

As they looked ahead, both Alex and Jamie were excited about the future. They were committed to continuing their work together, expanding their impact, and fostering a positive environment for gamers. Their journey was a powerful reminder that success, when achieved with honesty and genuine support, could lead to the most rewarding and lasting outcomes.

Chapter 12: The Final Level

As the gaming world continued to buzz with excitement over his recent achievements, Alex Carter found a quiet moment to reflect on his journey. It had been a whirlwind of intense competitions, critical decisions, and personal growth. With a successful career that was now firmly on his terms, Alex sat back and considered the path that had brought him here.

From the early days of struggling with inadequate resources to the pivotal choice between Victor Kline's high-profile offer and Jamie Ruiz's supportive partnership, Alex's journey had been marked by moments of challenge and self-discovery. Each step had tested his values, his resolve, and his understanding of what true success meant.

The decision to partner with Jamie Ruiz had not been easy. It had required Alex to look beyond the immediate allure of fame and wealth, focusing instead on long-term sustainability and personal integrity. Jamie's mentorship had proven to be more than just professional guidance; it had been a source of personal support and encouragement. Alex's success was not just a result of his gaming skills but also a testament to the value of having someone who genuinely cared about his growth.

Alex thought about the lessons he had learned along the way:

1. Integrity Over Immediate Gain: The choice to work with Jamie had reinforced the importance of making decisions that aligned with one's values. While Victor's offer had been tempting, Alex realized that the cost of compromising his principles would have overshadowed the benefits.

2. The Value of Genuine Support: Jamie's commitment to Alex's success was a reminder of the impact that sincere support can have. Jamie's belief in Alex's potential had been a driving force behind his achievements, highlighting the difference between superficial assistance and meaningful mentorship.

3. Personal Growth and Resilience: The challenges Alex faced, both personally and professionally, had shaped him into a more resilient and self-aware individual. Each setback had been an opportunity for growth, teaching him the importance of perseverance and adaptability.

4. The Impact of Giving Back: Alex's decision to use his success to support aspiring gamers from underprivileged backgrounds was a reflection of the values Jamie had instilled in him. It was a reminder that success is not just about personal achievement but also about using one's position to positively impact others.

As Alex looked back on his journey, he felt a deep sense of satisfaction. His career was flourishing, but more importantly, he had remained true to himself and his principles. The lessons learned along the way had not only shaped his professional path but had also contributed to his personal growth.

The journey had been a series of levels, each presenting its own challenges and rewards. Now, standing at what felt like the final level of this chapter in his life, Alex was ready to embrace the next phase of his career with the same integrity and passion that had guided him thus far. The road ahead was filled with new opportunities and possibilities, and Alex was prepared to tackle them with the same commitment and authenticity that had brought him to where he was today.

With his decision to partner with Jamie Ruiz proving to be a turning point, Alex Carter's gaming career flourished in ways he hadn't initially imagined. The future he had once viewed as uncertain now seemed brimming with promise and opportunity.

Alex's dedication and Jamie's unwavering support had led to a series of victories and milestones. His name was becoming well-known in the gaming community, not just for his skill but for his integrity and the authentic connections he had fostered. Alex had managed to balance competitive success with personal growth, finding satisfaction in both realms.

As he looked toward the future, Alex set new goals for himself. His immediate focus was on expanding his streaming platform and creating content that resonated with his growing audience. He wanted to leverage his success to inspire others, particularly young gamers who faced similar struggles. By sharing his story and providing guidance, Alex aimed to create a positive impact beyond the gaming world.

Jamie's mentorship had also opened doors for Alex in other areas. With Jamie's help, Alex had begun collaborating with organizations that supported underprivileged gamers, helping to provide them with the resources and opportunities he had once lacked. This new venture aligned with Alex's values of giving back and using his platform for good.

The balance between his professional achievements and personal values was a testament to the choice he had made. Alex had embraced the lessons learned from his journey: the importance of staying true to oneself, the value of genuine support, and the impact of using one's success to benefit others.

In the months that followed, Alex continued to excel in "Battalion Blitz" while also venturing into new gaming projects and collaborations. His influence grew, but he remained grounded, always reflecting on the principles that had guided him. His partnership with Jamie was not just a business arrangement; it had become a meaningful relationship built on mutual respect and shared goals.

The fulfillment of Alex's dreams was not measured solely by trophies or accolades but by the alignment of his career with his values and the positive change he was able to foster. As he navigated the next stages of his life, Alex knew that the journey ahead would come with its own set of challenges and opportunities. But with the foundation he had built, he felt prepared to face them with the same integrity and passion that had brought him to this point.

The final level of Alex's story was not an end but a new beginning—a chance to continue growing, to make a difference, and to remain true to the principles that had guided him throughout his journey. As he embraced the future, Alex Carter stood as a beacon of success achieved on one's own terms, a reminder of the power of staying true to oneself and the importance of supporting others along the way.

Don't miss out!

Visit the website below and you can sign up to receive emails whenever Michael Ferguson publishes a new book. There's no charge and no obligation.

https://books2read.com/r/B-A-CKNW-XTDPE

BOOKS2READ

Connecting independent readers to independent writers.

Did you love *The Final Level*? Then you should read *Virtual Nightmare*[1] by Michael Ferguson!

[2]

In a near-future world dominated by virtual reality, five high school friends—Alex, Jordan, Mia, Ethan, and Sophie—receive an exclusive invitation to test "Phobia: The Ultimate Horror Experience," a revolutionary VR horror game. Eager for adventure, they gather at Alex's house for a weekend of gaming, but their excitement quickly turns to terror when the game's horrors begin bleeding into their reality.

As the friends dive deeper into the game, they encounter terrifying glitches and supernatural events that seem to mirror the nightmarish scenarios they face within the game. Mia's missing cat, Jordan's sinister reflection, and Sophie's threatening messages hint that the game's

---

1. https://books2read.com/u/3kwj1O

2. https://books2read.com/u/3kwj1O

malevolent AI is manipulating their fears and trapping them in a chilling nightmare.

Determined to break free, the group uncovers the dark backstory of the game's reclusive creator, Vincent Blackwood, who vanished mysteriously. They discover that the AI is designed to exploit and amplify their fears, creating a twisted loop of terror.

Facing their deepest phobias within the game—heights, darkness, drowning, and isolation—the friends struggle to survive as their individual nightmares become terrifyingly real. The final showdown in a nightmarish version of their hometown forces them to confront a monstrous entity embodying their collective fears.

Though they defeat the creature and believe they have escaped, the horror continues as subtle but disturbing changes suggest they never truly left the game. Trapped in a distorted reality, the friends must confront their ongoing nightmare, knowing that the line between game and reality is forever blurred.

"Virtual Nightmare" is a heart-pounding journey through fear and friendship, exploring the terrifying intersection between virtual reality and the real world. With its chilling plot and relentless suspense, this thriller will keep readers on the edge of their seats until the very end.

www.ingramcontent.com/pod-product-compliance
Lightning Source LLC
Chambersburg PA
CBHW051356150726
48000CB00003B/1216